MONKEY NUT

For Erin, Isla and JP Parrot

SIMON AND SCHUSTER
First published in Great Britain in 2013 by Simon and Schuster UK Ltd
1st Floor, 222 Gray's Inn Road, London WC1X 8HB
A CBS Company
Text and illustrations copyright © 2013 Simon Rickerty
Elephant image copyright Felix Andrews in accordance with the GNU Free Documentation License
The right of Simon Rickerty to be identified as the author and illustrator of this work has been
asserted by him in accordance with the Copyright, Designs and Patents Act, 1988
All rights reserved, including the right of reproduction in whole or in part in any form
A CIP catalogue record for this book is available from the British Library upon request
ISBN: 978-0-85707-575-8 (HB)
ISBN: 978-0-85707-576-5 (PB)
ISBN: 978-0-85707-897-1 (eBook)

MONKEY NUT

by Simon Rickerty

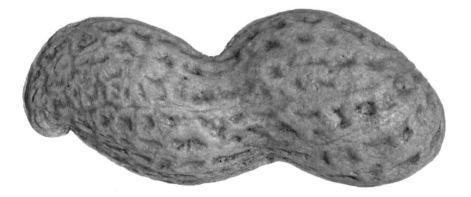

SIMON AND SCHUSTER
London   New York   Sydney   Toronto   New Delhi

eh?

It's my chair.

No, it's my chair.

It's my hat.

It's my telephone.

It's my rattle.

It's my drum.

It's my boat.

It's my skateboard.

WHEEEEEEE

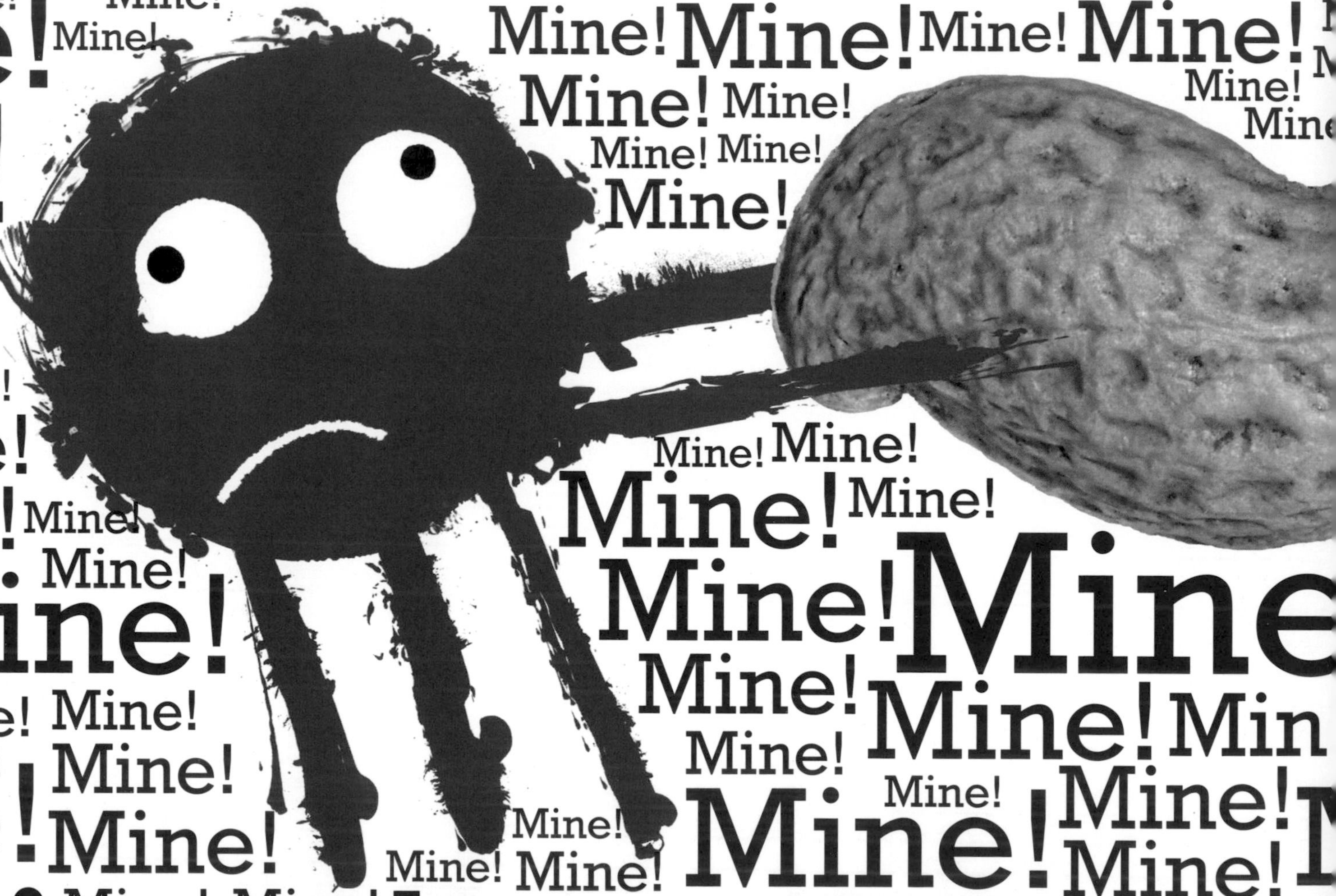

PING!

YUM!

MUNCH MUNCH!

MINE!